DOG MEETS DOG

Bernice Myers

I Like to Read®

HOLIDAY HOUSE • NEW YORK

I LIKE TO READ is a registered trademark of Holiday House Publishing, Inc.

This book has been officially leveled by using the F&P Text Level Gradient™ Leveling System.

Library of Congress Cataloging-in-Publication Data

Names: Myers, Bernice, author.
Title: Dog meets dog / Bernice Myers.
Description: First edition. | New York : Holiday House, [2019] | Series:
I like to read | Summary: Big Dog and Little Dog meet, become friends, and
have adventures together.
Identifiers: LCCN 2019014105 | ISBN 9780823444519 (hardcover)
Subjects: | CYAC: Dogs—Fiction. | Friendship—Fiction. | Snow—Fiction.
Classification: LCC PZ7.M9817 Do 2019 | DDC [E]—dc23
LC record available at https://lccn.loc.gov/2019014105

One day BIG DOG
and LITTLE DOG meet.

"Be my friend,"
says BIG DOG.

"What is a friend?"
says LITTLE DOG.

"Friends have fun,"
BIG DOG says.

"We can take a train
and go to the zoo."

"Or a bus . . .

to see the boats."

"Or a rocket to the moon!"
YES!

"Look, **BIG DOG**.
It is snowing,"
says LITTLE DOG.

BIG DOG runs home to wash.

LITTLE DOG runs home
to put on boots.

He wants to play
in the snow.

Oh, no!
LITTLE DOG falls.

Can you see him?

WOOF! WOOF! WOOF!

LITTLE DOG barks.

BIG DOG can hear LITTLE DOG.

Will he find LITTLE DOG
before it's too late?

LITTLE DOG is safe.

The next day the snow is gone.

The friends meet
in the park.

"Let's have some fun,"
says BIG DOG.
"On a train?"

"Too noisy,"
says LITTLE DOG.

"On a bus?"
says **BIG DOG**.

"Too bumpy,"
says LITTLE DOG.

"On a rocket
to the moon?"
says BIG DOG.

"Too far!"
says LITTLE DOG.

"Let's get ice cream!" they say.

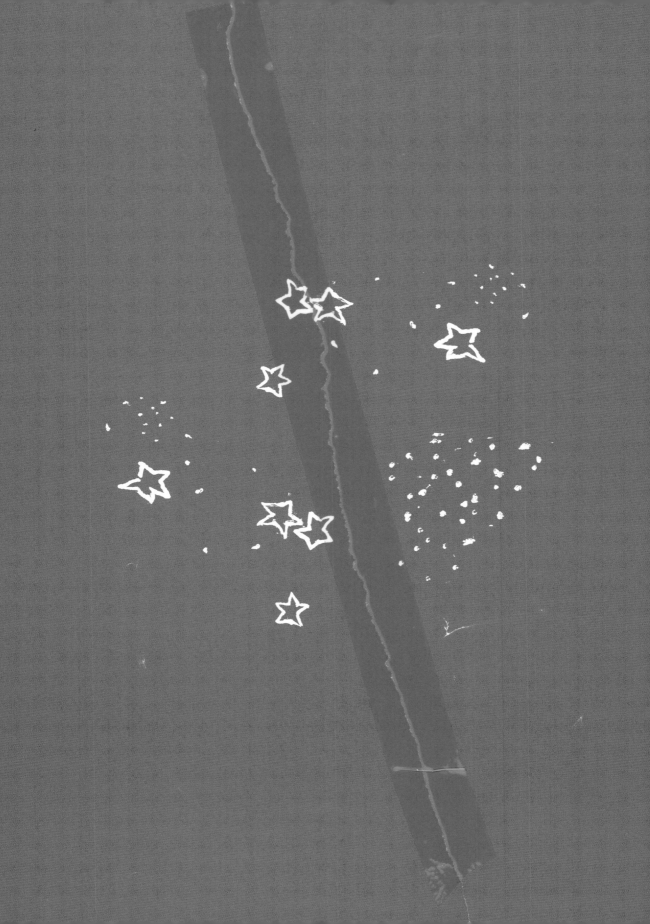